DISNEP
CLUB PENGUIN™

The Great Puffle Switch

PICK YOUR PATH 4

DISNEP
CLUB PENGUIN™
The Great Puffle Switch

PICK YOUR PATH 4

by Tracey West
Grosset & Dunlap
An Imprint of Penguin Group (USA) Inc.

GROSSET & DUNLAP
Published by the Penguin Group
Penguin Group (USA) Inc., 375 Hudson Street, New York,
New York 10014, USA
Penguin Group (Canada), 90 Eglinton Avenue East, Suite 700,
Toronto, Ontario M4P 2Y3, Canada
(a division of Pearson Penguin Canada Inc.)
Penguin Books Ltd., 80 Strand, London WC2R 0RL, England
Penguin Group Ireland, 25 St. Stephen's Green, Dublin 2, Ireland
(a division of Penguin Books Ltd.)
Penguin Group (Australia), 250 Camberwell Road, Camberwell,
Victoria 3124, Australia
(a division of Pearson Australia Group Pty. Ltd.)
Penguin Books India Pvt. Ltd., 11 Community Centre, Panchsheel Park,
New Delhi—110 017, India
Penguin Group (NZ), 67 Apollo Drive, Rosedale,
North Shore 0632, New Zealand
(a division of Pearson New Zealand Ltd.)
Penguin Books (South Africa) (Pty.) Ltd., 24 Sturdee Avenue,
Rosebank, Johannesburg 2196, South Africa

Penguin Books Ltd., Registered Offices:
80 Strand, London WC2R 0RL, England

© 2010 Disney. All rights reserved. Used under license by
Penguin Young Readers Group. Published by Grosset & Dunlap, a division of
Penguin Young Readers Group, 345 Hudson Street, New York, New York 10014.
GROSSET & DUNLAP is a trademark of Penguin Group (USA) Inc.
Printed in the U.S.A.

Library of Congress Cataloging-in-Publication Data is available.

ISBN 978-0-448-45331-6   10 9 8 7 6 5 4

"Hey, your puffle is cool!" says a pink penguin passing by.

"Thanks!" you say. You are walking into the Town Center with your green puffle, PJ. "PJ loves to go on walks. Don't you, PJ?"

PJ smiles at you. "Well, at least I *think* he does," you add, looking up at the pink penguin. "He always seems happy when we go out walking. Sometimes I wish he could talk so I would know exactly how he feels!"

The pink penguin nods. "Yeah, that would be awesome," she says. Then she waves. "I'm off to a soccer match. Bye!"

You wave back and then look down at PJ. "Okay, buddy. Where should we go now?"

PJ looks up at the sky. You follow his gaze and see black storm clouds in the sky. Then a drop of rain hits you right on the beak.

"Guess we should go inside somewhere," you say. "How about the Night Club?"

PJ hops up and down with excitement. You know that PJ loves to dance, so you head inside just as the rain begins to pour.

A pulsing beat is blasting from the speakers in the Night Club. Different colored spotlights shine on the penguins dancing on the dance floor. Some of them are wearing colorful outfits just right for dancing. You're wearing a T-shirt you got at the Music Jam party. PJ is wearing his red and white propeller hat. The two of you start to dance.

The propeller hat allows PJ to fly around. He zips and zooms around you, doing loops and whirls in the air.

"Go, PJ!" you yell. You're having a blast!

BoooooOOOOOOOM!

You nearly jump out of your skin as a loud clap of thunder rocks the Night Club. There is a sizzling sound as the lights flash on and off. You look over at PJ to see if he's okay, and see that he's hovering next to you. You reach out to grab him.

Suddenly . . . *Zap!* A jolt of light from the yellow spotlight hits PJ's propeller. PJ giggles. It tickles!

Zap! A jolt of bright pink light hits the propeller next.

Zap! Orange light. *Zap!* Green light. *Zap!* Blue light.

It happens so fast, you're not even sure it's

real. The colored streams of light rocket off
of PJ's propeller, and then they zap *you,*
knocking you backward!

You burst out in laughter as a funny, tingly
feeling hits you from the top of your head to the
bottom of your webbed feet. For a few seconds,
you can't see anything except for swirling yellow,
pink, orange, green, and blue lights.

Then the tickling feeling disappears.
You jump up.

"PJ, you okay?" you ask.

But PJ isn't hovering next to you anymore.
Instead, a green penguin is standing there.
A HUGE green penguin. You are very confused.

"I'm way better than okay!" the green
penguin says. "I feel amazing!"

"Excuse me," you say, "but I'm trying to find
my puffle, PJ."

The green penguin looks down. "Hey, boss.
Is that really you?"

"What do you mean?" you ask. "Do you
know me? And why are you so big?"

You try to gesture angrily at the penguin
with your flipper, and that's when you notice.

You don't have flippers anymore!

You slowly look down at your body. You
are round, green, and fuzzy. You have no flippers
or feet.

"This can't be true!" you yell. "I'm a puffle!"

"Sure looks that way," says the green
penguin. "And I'm a penguin!"

You take a closer look at the giant penguin
and realize he is wearing a T-shirt from the
Music Jam. *Your* T-shirt. The truth suddenly
hits you.

"No way!" you say. "PJ, you and I have
switched bodies!"

It can't be true, but it is. It's amazing,
exciting, and scary at the same time! Your mind
is full of questions.

"How did this happen?" you babble. "Must
have been when we were zapped by those lights.
Weird! How do we change back? And why am I
talking? Puffles can't talk!"

"Actually, we can," PJ says. "We talk to each
other. Penguins just can't understand us. I guess
I can understand you because I'm still really
a puffle, even though I'm in your body."

"I guess that makes sense," you say.

You never knew PJ was so smart!

"This is so cool!" PJ cries, dancing around. "Look at me! I have flippers! I can wear clothes!"

The other penguins on the dance floor are giving PJ strange looks. As cool as this whole accident is, it could be a problem. What if you stay trapped in PJ's body forever?

You wish there was someone smart enough to help you figure this out. Then it hits you—Gary the Gadget Guy! He's a supersmart inventor who's created some of the coolest things on Club Penguin. If anyone can help you, Gary can. You know that Gary has a workshop inside the Sport Shop. You should probably head there.

"PJ, come on," you say. "We need to get to the Sport Shop!"

PJ doesn't hear you. He's too busy trying out new dance steps, copying the penguins next to him.

You try to think what PJ does when he wants your attention. Then you remember. You start hopping up and down.

"PJ, come on!" you yell. "We have to go!"

PJ hears you. "Really? Do we have to?"

"Yes," you say. "Please?"

PJ nods. "Okay. Let's go."

You and PJ leave the Night Club. You hop alongside PJ as you follow the trail that leads to the Ski Village. PJ is sliding around on the icy path.

"Whoa! This is fun!" he says.

It is not easy to keep PJ focused on the way to the Sport Shop. He tries to touch everything he sees. He talks to every penguin he meets. When you pass a snow bank, he flops down in the snow and starts waving his flippers.

"Look! I'm making a snow angel!" he shouts happily.

You have to admit, that looks like fun. But unless you keep PJ moving, you'll never get there.

"It's beautiful, PJ," you say. "Now let's go!"

Finally you reach the Sport Shop. You follow PJ up the wooden steps. When you enter, PJ rushes over to a pair of skis on the wall.

"Cool!" he cries.

You hop over to the door of Gary's workshop. The door is closed, and you realize you have no way to knock or open the door.

"PJ, pick me up," you say.

PJ races over and lifts you up. That's when you notice the sign on the door:

Back soon—Gary

"He's not here," you grumble. "What should we do now?"

If you decide to wait for Gary to return, go to page 55.

If you go look for Gary, go to page 64.

CONTINUED FROM PAGE 52.

"Thanks so much," you say. "I wish we could help you, but I've got to find Gary."

Bouncer nods. "We understand. Good luck!"

"You too!" you say.

You look up at PJ. "Let's see if we can find Gary at the Cove."

You go to the Cove.

PJ's flippers flap with excitement as he sees all the penguins there having fun. Some are swimming, while others are gathered around the campfire listening to a penguin playing guitar. PJ forgets all about your mission to find Gary.

"I want to play *Catchin' Waves!*" he cries.

Before you can stop him, PJ grabs a surfboard and races into the water.

You watch from the shore as PJ finds his balance on the surfboard. He sees you and waves. Then he starts doing tricks—he even does a handstand.

"Woo-hoo!" he cries happily.

You know how PJ feels, because you think playing *Catchin' Waves* is a blast. You realize it must be hard for PJ to be stuck in your igloo while you are out having fun. If you ever get back into your own body, you promise yourself that you will take PJ for more walks.

PJ is dancing on his surfboard when a killer wave rises up behind him.

"Look out!" you cry, but it's too late. The wave washes PJ up onshore. He jumps to his feet, laughing.

"That was awesome!" he says. Then he points to a blue penguin examining a stack of surfboards. "Look! It's Gary."

You and PJ run up to Gary.

"Gary!" PJ yells. "I'm a puffle trapped inside my penguin's body and he's trapped in mine because we were in the Night Club and lightning struck and the lights went crazy!"

Another penguin might have thought PJ hurt his head when that wave hit him, but Gary nods seriously.

"How interesting," he says. "Why don't you two come back to my workshop with me so we can discuss this further?"

Go to page 80.

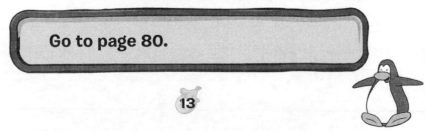

CONTINUED FROM PAGE 57.

Gary said to go to a high place, so you and PJ decide to ride the chair lift up to the Ski Hill. PJ holds out the little box and presses the red button. You hear a beep and see the words "Reading Completed" on the screen.

You and PJ head back to Gary. He's got the Monster Maker ready to go. All of the tubes and lights on the machine make you nervous, but Gary says not to worry. He places you on an X he's marked on the floor, and tells PJ to stand on another X.

Gary hits a switch and colored lights shoot out of the Monster Maker. The lights hit your propeller hat and then bounce off and hit PJ.

Just like before, your whole body tingles. When you open your eyes, you look down at your body and see that you are a penguin again!

You pick up PJ. "Gary did it!" you say.

You're glad it worked—but part of you is a little sad. Maybe your adventure ended too soon. After all, how many penguins get to be a puffle?

THE END

You check the Snow Forts first. When you get there, you see a blue puffle expertly throwing snowballs at the Club Penguin Clock Tower. Gary designed the clock with a snowball target attached to it. Every time the target gets hit by a snowball, the clock gets charged up.

The blue puffle hits the bull's-eye every time. You are impressed, and then you remember that even though you can't talk to penguins, you can talk to other puffles.

"Wow, you've got great aim," you say.

The blue puffle turns to you and smiles. "Thanks," she says. "I'm Bouncer."

"Nice to meet you," you reply. You decide not to tell Bouncer that you're a penguin in a puffle's body just yet. You don't want to freak her out. "I'm looking for Gary the Gadget Guy. Have you seen him?"

"You just missed him," Bouncer says. "He was fixing the clock, but then he took off."

You frown. "Guess I'll have to keep looking, then. Thanks a lot for your help!"

"Anytime," Bouncer says.

You decide to head for the Forest, but when you turn around, you discover PJ is nowhere in sight.

"Oh no!" you cry.

"What's the matter?" Bouncer asks.

"I lost my pu—my penguin," you say.

"Looks like you're having some bad luck," Bouncer says. "First you lost Gary, and now your penguin. I can help you out if you want."

You're starting to think that Bouncer is a very special puffle. Not only can she throw snowballs like a pro, but she's really nice, too.

"That would be great," you say. "But I'm not sure if I should find PJ first, or catch up with Gary. It's really important that I talk to him."

"I'll help you look, no matter what you decide," Bouncer says.

If you go after Gary, go to page 47.
If you go after PJ, go to page 78.

CONTINUED FROM PAGE 50.

"Buck up there, matey!" Blast says. "Bein' a puffle is a lot of fun."

"True," Flare agrees.

"Me and Flare'll show you how to have a grand old time as a puffle," Blast says. He lowers his voice. "In fact, my friends and I are throwin' a party for Yarr later in the hold of the *Migrator*. You should come."

"I didn't know puffles had parties," you say.

"Aye, we do!" Blast replies. He looks at you. "Puffles have secret parties all the time. Penguins never pay any attention. They're too busy with parties of their own."

"That's cool," you say. "I'll be there."

Blast winks. "The password is 'scallywag.' "

You spend the next few hours looking for PJ, but you can't find him anywhere. Then you head over to the *Migrator*. Penguins are walking up the gangplank to get into the ship. You hop over to a porthole on the ship's bottom. A black puffle's head pops out of the porthole.

"Password?" the puffle asks.

"Scallywag," you reply.

The puffle hops to the side and welcomes you inside the ship. You can't believe your eyes. Puffles of every color are inside the ship's hold. Black puffles are jumping over cream soda kegs on their skateboards. Purple puffles are blowing bubbles. Yellow puffles are playing the flute, and all the puffles are dancing to the music. You've never seen anything like it.

Then Blast hops over to you with a red puffle by his side.

"I'd like you to meet my good mate, Yarr," he tells you.

"Yarr!" you cry. "I can't believe I'm meeting you in person!"

"It's a pleasure to meet ye as well," Yarr says. "I was just telling Blast here about me latest adventure with the captain. Would ye like to hear it?"

"Of course I would!" you say, and you settle in to listen to the tale.

You don't feel so bad about temporarily losing PJ. Otherwise, you never would have been invited to this amazing puffle party!

THE END

CONTINUED FROM PAGE 34.

You and Bouncer decide to check out the Town Center first. The Night Club floor is really crowded. You see a green puffle bouncing on top of a speaker and ask if she's seen PJ, but she says she hasn't.

Just to be safe, you check the Dance Lounge upstairs. Then you and Bouncer check the Gift Shop and the Coffee Shop. You see lots of penguins, but no PJ.

"I think we can safely say that PJ's not here," Bouncer tells you. "We'd better get to the Ski Hill before it's too late."

You hop out of the Town Center, past the Dock, and take the path to the Ski Village. PJ is just about to get on the Ski Lift.

"PJ, finally!" you cry, hopping to him. "We have to get to Gary's workshop, quick."

"Can't I ride the lift some more?" PJ asks.

"Sorry," you say. "We're almost out of time."

You, PJ, and Bouncer enter the Sport Shop and hurry into Gary's workshop. The room is a mess of machine parts and crumpled papers. Gary is busily typing at his computer.

"I've been doing some calculations," Gary says when he hears you come in. "If my theory is correct, your molecular switch occurred during a precise alignment of barometric pressure and planetary forces."

You're not sure what Gary just said. All you want to know is, "Can we switch back?"

Gary looks at his watch. "Unfortunately, you're one minute too late. I'm very sorry."

You're shocked. Being a puffle is fun, but you miss your penguin body.

"Do I have to be a puffle forever?" you ask.

"Fortunately, no," Gary says. "The same conditions should occur in exactly one year."

"One year's not so bad," Bouncer says. "I bet you'll have fun as a puffle."

"I'll take care of you," PJ promises. "Let's go back to our igloo. We can arrange the puffle furniture to make you more comfortable."

You're touched. "Thanks, PJ," you say.

"And I'll come visit you," Bouncer says.

With friends like these guys, you could get used to being small, round, and furry!

THE END

CONTINUED FROM PAGE 69.

You and PJ leave the Iceberg and head back to the Sport Shop. Gary is in his workshop.

With the help of a puffle translating device that Gary uses, you explain what happened. Gary thinks the colored lights that hit you in the Night Club triggered the switch. He zaps you and PJ with colored laser lights he has. It works! The two of you switch bodies. You both thank Gary and head back to your igloo.

When you waddle inside your igloo, you are shocked at the sight in front of you. Your six new puffle friends are waiting for you in your igloo!

Bouncer is juggling snowballs. Flare is doing skateboard tricks. Chirp plays the flute while Pop blows bubbles. Loop twirls her lasso so it forms the words "Thank You!" Then Chirp shyly gives you a picture she has painted. It's you and PJ with the Elite Puffles!

You are amazed. "You guys rock! Let's turn up the music and party!"

THE END

CONTINUED FROM PAGE 66.

"Try going from three o'clock to two o'clock," you suggest.

Bouncer begins to throw snowballs into the holes. After she hits the twelfth target, the crystals begin to glow brighter.

You begin to tingle. *It's working!* you think. The tingling stops. You look down at yourself.

You are still round and fuzzy. But you're not green—you're blue! You look at Bouncer. She's green.

"I think we switched bodies," Bouncer says.

You nod. "You're right. Sorry about that."

Bouncer whips up some more snowballs. "Let me try it the other way."

She throws the snowballs in the other direction, but nothing happens.

Bouncer sighs. "Let's see. PJ's in your body. You're in my body. And now I'm in PJ's body."

"We should go find Gary," you say.

If Gary can't sort this out, you don't know what you'll do!

THE END

CONTINUED FROM PAGE 48.

"I guess we should play it safe," you say. "Let's go wait for PJ in your workshop."

Suddenly, you hear a high-pitched whistle.

"Sorry, guys," Bouncer says. "I'm needed for another mission. Good luck."

Bouncer hurries off before you can thank her. You're curious about her mission.

"Gary, how do you know her?" you ask.

Gary grins. "I'm afraid I can't say."

You and Gary head back to his workshop. The shelves are crammed with Gary's inventions. You look around, impressed.

"Are you interested in inventions?" Gary asks. "I'm working on a new one right now."

"I'd love to see it!" you say.

Gary takes what looks like a silver backpack off of a shelf. "It's a puffle jet pack," he says. "Green puffles can use a propeller hat to fly. But with this invention, all puffles can fly if they want to."

"Cool!" you say.

"I've been meaning to test it," Gary says. "Would you be interested in helping me?"

"Of course!" you say.

Gary straps the Puffle Power Pack to your back, and you whiz around his office. He times you for speed and measures your flight path.

PJ walks in during the test. "Sorry I wandered off!" he says. "Once I realized I lost you, I figured I'd come back here and wait for Gary."

You gently come to a landing on the floor. "Smart thinking, PJ."

Gary uses a Monster Maker device to switch you and PJ back into your bodies. It shoots out a bunch of crazy lights and doesn't hurt at all. It's just tingly and funny-feeling, like the first time. You're happy to be in your old body again.

"Thanks a lot, Gary," you say.

"You're welcome," Gary says. "If there's anything you ever need, just let me know."

"There is one thing," you ask shyly. "Could I have your autograph?"

"Why, certainly," Gary says.

You and PJ leave with a signed picture of Gary. You can't wait to show your friends!

THE END

CONTINUED FROM PAGE 73.

You shake the snow off of your fur. "Sorry, guys," you say. "Actually, I'm new at this. I'm really a penguin. I switched bodies with my puffle this morning. It's kind of a long story."

"Whoa, that's wild," Flare says.

"You can tell us about it later. Right now, we've got a mission to solve," Bouncer says with determination.

"Aye! Leave it to me!" Blast cries.

Blast shoots himself out of a tiny cannon, soaring high above the signpost. He spins in the air several times before he lands.

"Shiver me timbers, it's true! There's something green floatin' in the waters around the Iceberg," he says.

"Cool! Maybe it *is* a sea monster," Pop says, bouncing up and down with excitement.

Loop shivers. "Do you really think so?"

You and PJ race to the Iceberg with the Elite Puffles. When you arrive, you can clearly see something floating in the water, but it's not a sea monster. A green penguin is sitting on top of a wooden crate floating in the water.

The penguin waves frantically when she sees you onshore.

"She's pretty far out," Bouncer says. "We'll need to rescue her."

Loop jumps in with an idea. She looks at you. "I can tie myself to you. We can fly out, and then I'll lasso the penguin," she suggests.

"Not a bad idea, but this puffle's not so great with a propeller hat, remember?" Pop points out. "I have an idea. I can blow a big bubble and send it out to the penguin. Then we can both float back to shore."

"Good idea, but if it gets windy, we may lose you," Bouncer says. "I'm not sure what to do."

She looks at you. "What do you think? Are you ready to fly again?"

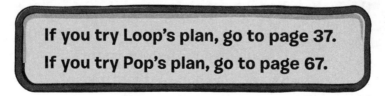

If you try Loop's plan, go to page 37.
If you try Pop's plan, go to page 67.

CONTINUED FROM PAGE 57.

"Let's go to the Beacon," you tell PJ.

You and PJ make your way to the Beach as a strong wind whips up.

The yellow glowing light of the Beacon shines against the dark clouds as you approach the Lighthouse. You step inside and a rock band is playing on the stage. PJ starts to dance, but you impatiently hop up and down.

"PJ! We've got to get that reading for Gary!"

PJ reluctantly follows you up the stairs to the top of the Lighthouse. A red puffle is looking through the telescope that looks out over the ocean. He turns when he hears you.

"Ahoy there, maties!" he cries. "What brings you here on this dark and stormy afternoon?"

"It's kind of a long story," you say. "This penguin here is actually my puffle, PJ. We switched bodies."

"Shiver me timbers!" the puffle cries. "My name's Blast, and that story's as exciting as anything I've read in Rockhopper's journal."

PJ runs up to the telescope. "Can I look through it? What can you see?"

27

Blast hops aside for PJ. "The *Migrator* is on the horizon," Blast says. "I can't wait to see Captain Rockhopper and my old friend, Yarr."

"Cool!" you say. You love it when Rockhopper visits. You hope you'll be in your penguin body before he gets here.

The sound of rumbling thunder fills the air.

"You'd better get that reading, PJ," you say. "It sounds like another storm is going to hit."

BOOM! A huge clap of thunder explodes above you. The air sizzles as a jagged streak of lightning shoots down from the sky. It hits the Beacon, shattering the glass around it!

Sparks shoot out from the glowing bulb, and then it fizzles out. The yellow glow fades. Blast looks really concerned.

"Blimey!" he cries. "Without the light of the Beacon, Rockhopper's ship will crash!"

Blast looks at you and PJ. "I know yer own mission is important, lads, but could you help me fix the Beacon, and save Rockhopper and Yarr?"

"Of course!" you and PJ reply.

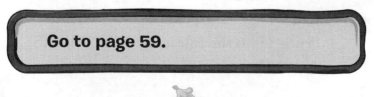

Go to page 59.

CONTINUED FROM PAGE 73.

"I'm sorry, guys," you say, shaking the snow off your fur. "You see, I'm not really a puffle. It's a long story. PJ and I should just leave. Come on, PJ, let's go."

"Don't go!" Bouncer calls out.

"Sorry," you say. "I just don't think I can fly the way you need me to. I don't want to interfere with your mission."

You and PJ head down the Ski Hill.

"Too bad that didn't work out, PJ," you say. "Let's go find Gary. PJ?"

You turn around—and PJ isn't behind you.

"PJ? Where are you?" you call out.

The Ski Village is crowded with penguins. You have to hop out of the way to avoid being stepped on and to make things worse, you don't see PJ anywhere.

You've got to find him. You head out of the Ski Village, not sure where you're going. You're feeling a little scared to be wandering on your own when you're so little.

Then you hear something—the sound of happy puffle voices. You raise your head and see a group of wild green puffles playing in the snow. They look so happy! A strange feeling comes over you. You may have the mind of a penguin, but you have the heart of a puffle. You race to join them.

"Hey! What are you guys doing?" you ask.

"We're playing tag," one of the green puffles replies. "Come on, play with us!"

You eagerly join the game. As you're playing, you notice that there is a lone white puffle in the group. He's shy, but really nice. You and the white puffle quickly become friends.

You spend the next few days with the band of wild puffles playing games, eating Puffle-O Berries, and sleeping huddled together in one big, fuzzy pile. You start to feel less like a penguin trapped in a puffle's body, and more like a real puffle. It just feels so right!

A few weeks later, you and your puffle friends are in the Forest, playing tag. You're hiding behind a tree when you see a penguin walk by. The penguin looks awfully familiar.

Then you realize who it is! It's PJ, still in your penguin body. You hop out. You've found PJ at last!

At that moment, your friend the white puffle hops behind you, bumping into you.

"Tag! You're it!"

You start to chase after your puffle friend, but stop in your tracks. If you leave PJ now, you may never find him again.

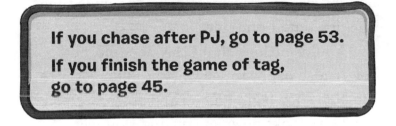

If you chase after PJ, go to page 53.
If you finish the game of tag, go to page 45.

You think the tracks might be important. So you and Bouncer follow them to a small, open field where you see Gary the Gadget Guy fiddling with a strange machine. It's a metal box the size of a refrigerator with a wide tube sticking out of one side.

You're curious about the machine, but you're also happy to see Gary. You hop over to him and start bouncing up and down.

Gary looks down at you and Bouncer through his round eyeglasses.

"Hello, Bouncer," he says. He takes a small black box out of his pocket and turns it on. "Good thing I have my puffle translator with me."

"My new friend here needs your help," says Bouncer. "And I'm also investigating the mysterious disappearance of Puffle-O Berries from some bushes nearby."

"How do you know each other?" you ask.

"Bouncer is an Elite Puffle. He is one of a few select puffles who helps the Elite Penguin Force," Gary explains.

"I didn't even know puffles could do that!" you say, impressed.

Bouncer smiles. "It's a thrill," she says. "I've got some great stories to tell you. But now, we've got some problems to solve. Gary, is that a wind machine?"

Gary nods. "Why, yes, it is."

"Have you been testing it?" Bouncer asks.

Gary nods. "It produces a strong wind."

You think you know what Bouncer is getting at. "Strong enough to blow Puffle-O Berries off of their bushes?" you ask.

"Why, yes," Gary replies. "Oh my, did that happen? I am so sorry. I will find another place to test my machine."

He starts to pack up the machine, but you stop him. "Before you go, Gary, I need your help," you say. "You see, I'm not really a puffle. I'm a penguin in a puffle's body."

"Really?" Bouncer asks.

"That's quite remarkable," Gary says. "Please tell me what happened."

You explain the whole story.

"And where is PJ now?" Gary asks.

"I don't know," you say. "He wandered off."

Gary frowns. "That could be a problem. I have seen this phenomenon once before. If you don't switch bodies with PJ within an hour, you may be trapped in each other's bodies forever."

Forever? You don't like the sound of that.

"Yikes," you say. "So what should I do?"

"I will go back to the Sport Shop and get things ready to switch you back," Gary says. "Find PJ and bring him to my workshop."

Gary hurries off. You look at Bouncer.

"Club Penguin is a big place. I don't even know where to start!" you say.

"A lot of puffles I know love to slide down the Ski Hill," Bouncer says. "PJ might be there."

You nod. "PJ loves to dance. Maybe he went into the Town Center to go to the Night Club."

"Those are both good choices," Bouncer says. "Let's pick one and get there fast."

If you head into the Town Center, go to page 19.

If you go to the Ski Hill, go to page 62.

CONTINUED FROM PAGE 61.

You are really impressed by your new puffle friends, and you want them to be impressed by you, too.

"I can do this," you say confidently.

"Hop to it, then, mate!" Blast says.

You put your propeller hat on and grab the handle of the gas can in your mouth. The propeller spins, lifting you off of the ground.

You fly toward the penguin in the boat. But the gas can is heavier than you thought it would be, and you fizzle out halfway across the water.

"Uh-oh!" you cry out, as you and the gas can land in the water with a splash.

You try to swim to shore when you remember you don't have flippers anymore—you can't swim! Just then, a strong wave lifts you up. You hold your breath as the wave washes over you. It dumps you back on shore next to PJ and the other puffles.

"Uh, sorry," you say. "I guess you were right. I'm not ready to do this yet."

"Don't sweat it. That was mighty brave!" Blast says. "Now I'll give it a try."

You know that red puffles can shoot themselves out of a cannon, and Blast is no different. He picks up another gas can and hops inside his cannon.

Boom! The cannon sends Blast flying across the water. He lands perfectly inside the boat.

"Awesome landing," says the penguin, shaking his head in amazement. He takes the gas can and fills the tank of the Hydro-Hopper. Soon the boat comes chugging back to the Dock, and Blast hops off.

"Thanks!" the grateful penguin says.

Blast turns to the rest of you. "We must hurry back to the Beacon, lads, or else our mateys Rockhopper and Yarr are in trouble!"

You all rush back to the Beacon. Rain falls on all of you as Flare examines the fried wires. Then he begins to weld them together with the fiery energy stored in his body.

The rain comes down harder. A strong wind whips up. You gasp as the wind picks up Flare, carrying him away!

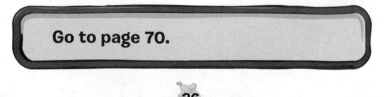

Go to page 70.

CONTINUED FROM PAGE 26.

"I think I can do it," you say.

"Hooray!" cries Loop, as a big smile appears on her fluffy pink face.

PJ waddles over to you. "Let me give you a tip," he says. "The propeller lifts you up, but you have to lean left, right, backward, or forward to move exactly where you want to go."

You nod. "Got it."

Loop wraps her rope around the two of you. You pop on your propeller hat.

The propeller starts to spin, lifting you off the ground. You remember PJ's advice and lean slightly forward. It works! The propeller carries you across the water. You're halfway to the penguin when Loop calls up to you.

"This is close enough," she says, taking out another rope and twirling it in the air. Then she tosses the lasso to the stranded penguin, wrapping it around her body.

"Let's head back," Loop tells you.

But carrying two puffles and one penguin is a lot of work for one small propeller hat. You try, but you can't lift the penguin off of the crate.

"I'll jump in the water," the penguin offers. "I'm not a great swimmer, but you can pull me along. I'll be fine."

This sounds like a good idea. You fly back to shore as the penguin paddles with her flipper and Loop pulls her along. When you finally land, you're exhausted but proud of what you've done.

The green penguin looks at PJ. "Your puffles saved me. Thanks."

"Hey, PJ," you say. "Can you find out what happened to this penguin?"

PJ nods. "So, how did you end up all the way out there?" he asks the green penguin.

"I fell asleep on the Beach," she replies. "The next thing I knew, a wave carried me out into the water. Luckily, that crate floated by and I climbed on. I don't know what I would have done if you guys hadn't helped me."

"We're happy to help," PJ says. "Now, get yourself to the Town Center and drink some cocoa. You could use it."

The rescued penguin waves and walks away. Bouncer is staring at the crate. "I wonder what's in that crate," she says. "Could be something important. It looks heavy."

Pop jumps up and down with excitement. "Oh, my turn! My turn!" she says.

She rushes to the shore and blows a huge bubble. Then she puffs on it, and it floats across the water and surrounds the crate. The crate floats up and over the water and lands onshore.

"The crate is covered in ice," says Bouncer.

Chirp bounces up. "That's nothing some beautiful music can't fix," says the yellow puffle. She takes out a flute and plays a loud, high-pitched tone. The ice cracks and flies off in pieces. Chirp grins.

"Supersonic sound waves," she tells you.

You are really impressed with these Elite Puffles. They have amazing talents!

Flare hops up to the crate and whips out a welding torch. "I'll have these locks off in a minute, dudes."

You, PJ, and the Elite Puffles gather around as Flare removes the metal locks. All of you wonder: What could possibly be inside?

Go to page 46.

CONTINUED FROM PAGE 48.

"We should go to the cave in the name of science," you tell Gary. "We have to wait for PJ, anyway. We might as well give the cave a try."

"Very well," Gary says. He hands you a map showing the way to the cave.

You thank Gary, and you and Bouncer follow the map into the mountains. You spot a hole at the bottom of one of the hills.

"We found the cave!" Bouncer says. She quickly bounces toward the cave's entrance.

It's dark inside the cave, but there is enough sunlight to see two tunnels ahead of you. You look at the map. But it doesn't show any tunnels.

"Then I guess we have two choices," Bouncer says. "We can go into the tunnel on the left or the tunnel on the right."

If you take the left tunnel, go to page 65.

If you take the right tunnel, go to page 74.

CONTINUED FROM PAGE 79.

"Let's follow Flit," you suggest. "The tracks will still be here later."

You put on your own propeller hat to catch up to the green puffle. He flies around another small hill and you gasp as you turn the corner. There's a huge pile of Puffle-O Berries!

"The Puffle-O Berries arc here!" you cry out.

Bouncer comes hopping around the bend. She looks up at Flit.

"Flit! Did you do this?" Bouncer asks.

"Nope," Flit replies.

Suddenly the pile of berries shifts, and a green penguin pops up. It's PJ! His mouth is stuffed with Puffle-O Berries.

"You penguins can keep your pizza," PJ says. "Nothing is as delicious as Puffle-O Berries!"

Bouncer smiles. "It looks like we solved two problems at once. We found the Puffle-O Berries, and your penguin, too."

You decide to tell Bouncer the truth. "Actually, PJ's not my penguin. He's my puffle."

You explain to Bouncer and Flit how you and PJ switched bodies.

"We need Gary to change us back," you say.

Bouncer looks thoughtful. "Hmm. Maybe you don't need Gary. An electrical storm caused you to switch bodies, right? Then maybe an electrical storm can change you back."

You look up at the sky. It's blue with a few puffy white clouds hanging there. "Who knows when the next storm will be?"

Two more puffles hop up, a yellow one and a pink one. Flit flies over to them.

"Hey, Chirp. Hey, Loop," he says.

"What's all this talk about a storm?" asks Chirp, the yellow puffle.

"We need to make one," Bouncer says.

"Sounds good!" says Loop, the pink puffle.

Make a storm? The four puffles huddle together, and once again you get the feeling that they are not ordinary puffles. Flit flies up and nods to you.

"Follow my lead," Flit says.

Flit starts to fly around the pile of Puffle-O Berries, and you follow him. The two of you fly faster and faster until you create a whirlwind. Then Flit yells out, "Break away!"

You fly out of the whirlwind, and the

wind breaks free, sending the Puffle-O Berries scattering over the hills. Happy wild puffles bounce toward them, eager to eat.

"My turn," Bouncer says. She starts throwing snowballs at the clouds.

Wham! Wham! Wham! One after another. The clouds begin to look dark and heavy.

Chirp hops next to Bouncer. "If I play my flute at the correct frequency, not only will it sound beautiful and amazing, but it should create a spectacular electrical charge, too."

Chirp plays a song on the flute. The air begins to crackle with electricity.

"We need the colors now, Chirp," Bouncer reminds her.

"Of course," Chirp says. She whips out a paint palette and begins to paint five circles of color: yellow, pink, orange, green, and blue.

"Those are just like the colored spotlights in the Night Club that hit us," you say.

Then Loop twirls a lasso over her head. A streak of jagged lightning shoots down from the sky, and Loop lassos it!

"Yee-ha!" she cries. She whips the lasso and aims the lightning at Chirp's colored circles.

Yellow! Pink! Orange! Green! Blue! The lightning changes color and zaps you in your propeller hat, then bounces off and hits PJ.

Your whole body tingles. You look down. You are not round and fluffy. You have feet and flippers. You are back in your own body!

Loop lets go of the lasso, and the lightning fizzles out. The sky clears.

"It worked!" you cry. "I don't how you did it. You're not ordinary puffles, are you?"

The puffles look at each other and smile. You realize you can't understand them anymore, and that makes you a little sad.

Then Chirp gives you something: It's a sculpture of a puffle. You know Chirp is artistic, so you guess she made it herself.

The base of the sculpture reads: "You are hereby named an Honorary Puffle."

"Wow, thanks," you say.

You bend down and pick up PJ.

"Let's go home, buddy," you say.

PJ smiles. Even though you can't understand him, you know he's happy.

THE END

CONTINUED FROM PAGE 31.

You watch PJ disappear around the bend. Part of you wants to talk to him, but if you do, you know that PJ will probably want to switch bodies with you.

The thing is, you're not sure if you want to. Being a puffle is the most fun you've ever had. You get to be wild and free, with no responsibilities. And you love your new puffle friends.

"Hey! Aren't you gonna catch me?" the white puffle yells.

You smile and hop toward him. "You'd better hop fast! I'm on my way!"

Then you hop off after your puffle friend, leaving your life as a penguin behind you forever.

THE END

CONTINUED FROM PAGE 39.

Flare opens the crate and you all gasp. It's loaded with cool tiki mugs!

"We've got to share these with all of the penguins on the island," Bouncer says. "First, tell us how you and your puffle switched places."

You explain the story. "It seems to me that the sequence of lights that struck you and PJ caused the switch," she says. "Maybe we can recreate that."

You head to the Night Club. Bouncer instructs you and PJ to go to the exact spots you were at on the dance floor. You put on your propeller hat. Flare finds a control panel for the lights on the wall and goes to work.

Then, the lights zap your propeller cap and hit PJ. Your body tingles. When it's all over, you're a penguin again.

You thank Bouncer and offer to help distribute the tiki mugs. Luckily, you can still understand puffle language, thanks to your time as a puffle!

THE END

CONTINUED FROM PAGE 16.

"I think we should try to find Gary," you say.

"Sure," says Bouncer. She nods toward a path. "Let's go that way."

You hop down the path and you're in luck—you see a blue penguin in a white lab coat walking there. It's Gary!

Gary smiles when he sees the two of you.

"Why hello, Bouncer," he says.

You wonder how Gary knows Bouncer. But before you can ask, Gary takes a little black box out of his pocket and turns it on.

"This is my puffle translator. It's a new invention of mine. Now, what are you two puffles up to?"

Bouncer nods toward you. "Ask greenie."

You take a deep breath. "I have something to tell you— both of you," you say, looking at Bouncer. "I am a penguin in a puffle's body."

Gary and Bouncer listen intently as you tell your story.

"That's amazing!" Bouncer says when you are finished.

"Quite," Gary agrees. He taps his chin

thoughtfully. "I may know a way to switch you back. However, we'll need your puffle for that. Where is he?"

"I don't know," you say. "He wandered off."

"I have two suggestions," Gary says. "You could go back to my workshop and see if your puffle turns up there. Or . . ." his voice trails off.

Gary shakes his head. "I shouldn't even mention it," he says. "I have heard a rumor that two penguins once discovered a cave in the mountains. Something happened in the cave that caused the penguins to switch bodies. If this rumor is true, this cave may hold the answer to your problem."

You hop up and down in excitement. "That sounds perfect! Where is this cave?"

Gary frowns. "I hesitate to tell you. It may be a wild goose chase."

If you go back to the Sport Shop and wait, go to page 23.

If you convince Gary to tell you where the cave is, go to page 40.

CONTINUED FROM PAGE 61.

Blast is probably right—you don't know how to fly with the propeller hat on.

"You can do it, Blast," you say.

"Arr!" Blast cries. "I'm on my way!"

Like all red puffles, Blast can shoot himself out of a cannon. He picks up a gas can in his mouth and hops inside the cannon. Then he lights the fuse and . . .

BAM! Blast shoots across the water and expertly lands in the boat. The penguin fills up the gas tank and the boat chugs back to the Dock. The grateful penguin climbs out.

"Thanks! I can't believe I was just saved by a puffle! You're awesome," he tells Blast.

This penguin is your good friend Sam! You're happy to see him, so you hop over to him.

"Hi, Sam! It's me!" you say, but he doesn't understand puffle language.

"Aw, someone wants attention!" Sam says, looking at you. "Hi, little guy." Sam pats you on the head. Then he spots PJ playing in the snow. "Hey there, buddy! Want to go play *Find Four*?"

"I've always wanted to do that!" PJ replies.

"What do you mean?" Sam asks. "We play that game all the time."

PJ and Sam take off, and you are tempted to chase after him—but you decide that helping to fix the Beacon is more important. You hurry to the Beacon with Blast and Flare. Flare fixes the Beacon by welding the fried wires.

"Ahoy there!" Blast cries out, looking through the telescope. "The *Migrator* is safely ashore!"

"That's great news," you say. "It's been great meeting you guys. But I've got to go to the Ski Village and find PJ. He's playing *Find Four* there."

"We'll help you find him," Blast says. "After all, you helped us!"

Blast and Flare accompany you to the Ski Village. But there's no sign of PJ anywhere. You realize he could be anywhere on the island by now.

You sigh. "I guess I'll have to be a puffle for a little while longer," you tell Blast and Flare.

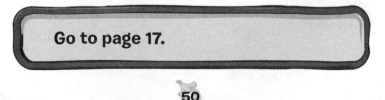

Go to page 17.

"Let's try the Forest," you say.

You and PJ go straight there. You don't see any penguins around. But you do see six puffles huddled in a circle, talking. There is a blue one, a red one, a black one, a yellow one, a pink one, and a purple one. As you hop closer to ask if they've seen Gary, you overhear their conversation.

"We need to come up with a plan," the blue puffle is saying. "This is an important mission."

A mission? What kind of mission could a bunch of puffles be going on?

The black puffle spots you and P.J. "We've got company," he says to his friends.

"I overheard you talking about your mission," you say. "I'm on a mission, too!"

The pink puffle smiles at you. "Are you working for the EPF?"

"The EPF?" you ask.

"The Elite Penguin Force," the blue puffle tells you. "They're a top secret branch of secret agents. They use Elite Puffles like us to help them. My name is Bouncer."

"Ahoy there! I'm Blast," says the red puffle.

"The name's Flare," the black puffle says, as he briefly transforms into a fiery ball of flames.

"I'm Chirp," the yellow puffle says. She plays a note on her flute. *Tweet!*

"They call me Loop," says the pink puffle, twirling a lasso in the air. "Nice to meet you!"

"What's up? I'm Pop!" says the purple puffle.

You introduce yourself and PJ. "We're on a mission to find Gary the Gadget Guy," you say. "Have you seen him?"

"No," Bouncer replies. "We'd help you, but we've got an important mission to complete."

"We could use some extra help," says Pop. "Do you want to join us?"

You are thrilled at this idea. But then you remember—you have a mission of your own, to find Gary. If you don't find him, you and PJ might never switch bodies.

If you decide to keep looking for Gary, go to page 12.

If you join the EPF mission, go to page 72.

CONTINUED FROM PAGE 31.

"Hang on!" you yell to your friend. "I've got to go do something."

You quickly hop after PJ and catch up to him on the path leading to the Plaza.

PJ sees you. His eyes grow wide with surprise. He reaches down and picks you up.

"I've been looking everywhere for you!" he says. "Have you been all right?"

"I've been fine," you tell him. "I met this great group of wild puffles."

That's when your friend the white puffle hops up to join you.

"What's going on?" he asks. "How come this penguin understands you?"

"It's sort of a long story," you say. "You see, I'm not really a puffle. I'm a penguin and I switched bodies with my puffle, PJ."

The white puffle looks up at PJ. "So that's really *you*? That's so weird."

"Can we go find Gary now?" PJ asks. "I like being a penguin, but I miss being a puffle."

"I know how you feel," you say. "Being a puffle is great, but I think we should switch back."

All three of you head to Gary's office, where PJ explains the situation to him. Gary does some calculations and uses his Monster Maker invention to create an electrical charge that switches you and PJ back into your own bodies.

"Thanks, Gary," you say, when it's all over. "You're a total genius."

You look down at PJ, who is a fluffy green puffle once again. But the white puffle looks sad.

"What's the matter?" you ask.

"I'm going to miss you," he says.

"Hey, wait a minute!" you say. "I can understand you!"

"Interesting," Gary muses. "You did spend several weeks in a puffle's body. That may explain why you know the language."

"Cool," you say. "Hey, do you want to come live with PJ and me?"

The white puffle brightens. "I'd love to!"

You head back to your igloo with your two puffles and the ability to speak the puffle language. What an awesome adventure!

THE END

CONTINUED FROM PAGE 11.

PJ is now happily bouncing up and down on a big pink exercise ball. You remember how distracted he was on the walk over here and decide it's safest to wait for Gary.

Luckily, Gary walks into the shop a minute later, wearing a white lab coat over his shirt and tie. The lenses of his round eyeglasses are fogged up from the wet weather outside. He hurries past you on the way to the door of his workshop.

You hop in front of him. "Excuse me!" you say. "Gary, I need your help!"

Gary looks down at you, smiling. "Well, aren't you an excited little puffle?" he says.

Oh no! Gary can't understand you. You start bouncing up and down more frantically.

Gary looks over at PJ, who is trying on a pair of ski boots—on his head.

"Hmm," Gary says. "Something unusual is going on here. Wait one moment."

Gary goes into his workshop and comes out with a small black box made of metal. He clips it onto his lab coat and turns a tiny dial on the device. The metal box squeaks and beeps.

"It's my latest invention—it allows me to translate the puffle language," he says. "Now please, go ahead and tell me what's wrong."

"I need your help, Gary," you say. "I switched bodies with my puffle, PJ!"

Gary doesn't seem shocked by this. "Fascinating!" he says. "That would explain your penguin—I mean puffle's—strange behavior. Please tell me how it happened."

You tell Gary the whole story, explaining that you switched bodies after the spotlights in the Night Club went crazy, zapping PJ's propeller hat and then striking you.

"Extremely interesting," Gary says thoughtfully. "The precise pattern of electric energy seems to have caused some kind of molecular switch. If we can replicate the pattern, it may be possible to switch you back."

Gary pulls a notebook and pen out of his pocket and starts furiously drawing calculations. Finally he looks down at you.

"Follow me," he says. "I have an idea."

You turn to PJ. "Hey, PJ, come on!"

PJ slips out of the inner tube he has put on and follows you into Gary's workshop. The place is a mess of shelves filled with strange devices and gadgets. Gary's desk is covered with papers.

Gary opens a cabinet and takes out another small black device. This one looks like a radio.

"A few Halloweens ago, I made a Monster Maker that attracts lightning storms," he says. "It can recreate the conditions that caused you and PJ to switch bodies. But first, I need a reading of the electromagnetic ions in the air."

"What do I do?" you ask.

"Just take this box to a high place and press the red button," Gary says. "Then bring it back to me, and I'll program the Monster Maker and change you back."

"No problem," you say. "But give it to PJ to hold. I have no hands!"

You and PJ walk outside the Sport Shop. Where should you take the box?

If you go to the Ski Hill, go to page 14.
If you go to the Beacon, go to page 27.

CONTINUED FROM PAGE 71.

You decide not to take a chance.

"Thanks, but we'll wait until the Monster Maker is fixed," you say.

You are glad you made that choice. Gary takes two weeks to repair the machine. While waiting, Blast and Flare teach you everything about being a puffle. You master flying with your propeller and eat lots of Puffle-O Berries, a puffle's favorite food.

PJ has fun being a penguin. He plays every game he can and tries on every outfit you own.

Two weeks pass by quickly. When the machine is fixed, Gary turns it on, the lights flash, and you're back in your old body.

"That was fun, wasn't it?" you ask. PJ nods.

You're glad to be a penguin again. Now you can talk to your buddies and train to be a ninja like you've always wanted. But sometimes you find yourself looking at the sky, hoping for a storm. You wouldn't mind being a puffle again—just for a little while.

THE END

CONTINUED FROM PAGE 28.

"I knew I could count on you two," Blast says. He hops around the Beacon, examining it. "Hmm. That lightning strike fried these wires like a platter of fish. We're going to need someone with skills to fix this. And I know just the puffle."

You follow Blast as he hops down the stairs into the Lighthouse.

"My good friend Flare can weld new wires for the Beacon," Blast explains. "We should be able to find him at the Sports Rink."

You all hurry to the Sports Rink, where you see a small group of black puffles skateboarding on the bleachers. The wind and the rain don't seem to bother them at all.

One of the black puffles zooms across the top bleacher on his skateboard. He rides off of the side, flips in midair, and lands smoothly in front of you. You are impressed.

"Yo, Blast," he says. "What's up, bro?"

"We've got a whale of a problem at the Beacon," Blast replies. "Lightning struck, and now there's no light, and the *Migrator*'s making her way to shore."

"Fried wires?" Flare asks. Blast nods. "I can handle that, no prob."

Flare turns to his friends. "Catch you later, dudes."

Flare rides his skateboard as you all head back to the Lighthouse. "So, who are these guys?" he asks Blast.

"Just wait till you hear this!" Blast says. "That penguin is actually PJ, a puffle, and this green puffle is really his penguin!"

"Whoa," says Flare.

"Nice to meet you," you say.

The four of you walk along the shore on the way back to the Lighthouse. Suddenly, you hear a cry from the water.

"Help! Help!"

A penguin is in the Hydro-Hopper, bobbing up and down on the waves.

"The boat ran out of gas!" he calls out. "The waves are pulling me away from shore. Can you help?"

You spot some gas cans on the Dock, and you get an idea.

"I can fly out to the boat with my propeller

hat and bring him a gas can," you suggest.

"Are ya sure ya can handle it?" Blast asks. "You've only just got used to bein' a puffle. I can get the gas can out there."

"How about the penguin dude? He could take a boat out there," Flare suggests.

You glance over at PJ. He's still overwhelmed with all the things he can do with his penguin body, and he's busy bouncing a beach ball. You don't think he can handle the task. It's got to be you or Blast.

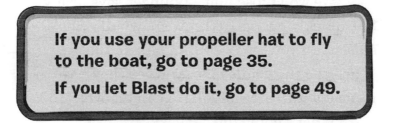

If you use your propeller hat to fly to the boat, go to page 35.

If you let Blast do it, go to page 49.

CONTINUED FROM PAGE 34.

You and Bouncer decide to check out the Ski Hill first. You hop on the Ski Lift and ride it to the top of the hill. To your relief, you spot PJ!

You quickly hop off the Ski Lift. "Hey, PJ!" you call out. "It's me!"

PJ doesn't hear you. A bunch of penguins are lining up for a Sled Race, and PJ joins them.

"Oh no," you say. "Once PJ gets to the bottom of that hill, we'll lose him again."

"We won't lose him," Bouncer says firmly. She quickly begins to throw snowballs. She's so fast, all you see is a white blur in the air. When the snowballs land, you see they have formed a wall around PJ. He can't move!

"What's going on?" PJ asks.

"We've got to get to the Sport Shop," you say. "If we don't switch bodies soon, we may be stuck in the wrong bodies forever."

PJ frowns. "You mean I'll never get to fly in a propeller hat again?"

"No, that's why we have to hurry."

PJ nods. "Being a penguin is really fun. But I am a puffle at heart. Let's go."

PJ knocks down the wall of snowballs, and you all take the Ski Lift down to the Sport Shop. Gary is waiting in his workshop for you. He's standing next to a strange-looking machine.

"Just in time," he tells you. "Ideally, we would need to create a lightning storm to replicate the charge that caused you to switch bodies. Luckily, I created this Monster Maker one Halloween. It should have the same effect."

You notice that Gary has plugged a row of colored lights into the Monster Maker.

"Please put on your propeller hat," he says.

You do as Gary says, and then he presses a switch and the lights start flashing. It's just like what happened in the Night Club. The lights flash, and your whole body feels ticklish. When it's all over, you are back in your own body.

"Wow, that's amazing!" you say. "Thanks so much, Gary. And you too, Bouncer. You really helped us."

"You are a lucky penguin," Gary tells you.

"I know. I got to find out what it's like to be a puffle. I still can't believe it happened!"

THE END

Waiting for Gary makes you impatient. You and PJ go look for Gary.

Outside, you see a bunch of penguins walking around. You walk up to a penguin wearing a Tour Guide hat.

"Have you seen Gary?" you ask her. But the Tour Guide walks right past you. Then you remember—you're a puffle! Penguins don't understand you. PJ will have to help you, but he's trying to climb onto the Ski Lift.

"PJ, not now," you say. "We have to find Gary. Ask around to see if anyone's seen him."

"Okay," PJ says. PJ talks to two different penguins. One thinks he saw Gary at the Snow Forts. Another says she saw him in the Forest.

You're not sure where to go. The Snow Forts are closer, but the Forest seems like a sure thing.

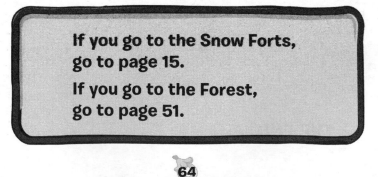

If you go to the Snow Forts, go to page 15.

If you go to the Forest, go to page 51.

CONTINUED FROM PAGE 40.

"Let's take the tunnel on the left," you suggest.

Bouncer agrees and follows you into the left tunnel. You walk down a dark path and begin to worry that it doesn't lead anywhere. Then the path opens up into an underground chamber.

You gasp. Glowing crystals line the walls of the chamber, bathing it in a soft glow. Mounds of snow are piled up on the cave floor, and you wonder how the snow got there.

"Look at the snow!" Bouncer says. "I could make some awesome snowballs with that stuff!"

There is a large wall in front of you with several snowball-sized holes carved into it, forming a circle. Above the circle of holes is an inscription:

Throw the snowballs one by one.
Start at three o'clock and follow the sun.
Follow the circle without a hitch,
and you can undo the switch.

"This must be it!" you cry. "The penguin who told Gary the story was telling the truth. We just have to do what the rhyme says."

"Okay," Bouncer says. "I guess we have to throw snowballs into the holes, one at a time. That's no problem for me. I'll hit every target. But where should I start?"

You gaze at the circle of holes for a minute. You realize there are twelve holes—just like there are twelve numbers on a clock.

"I think I know," you say. "The three o'clock hole is the hole where the number three should be on a clock. That's where you should start."

Bouncer nods. "That makes sense. But what does it mean, 'follow the sun'? The sun rises in the east and sets in the west. To travel east, I'd have to hit the two o'clock hole next."

"But then you'd be going back in time," you say. "The sun moves forward. I think you should throw it in the four o'clock hole next."

Bouncer frowns. "Both of these are good possibilities. Which one should we choose?"

If you think Bouncer should go from three to two o'clock, go to page 22.

If you think Bouncer should go from three to four o'clock, go to page 77.

CONTINUED FROM PAGE 26.

"Maybe it's better if Pop does it," you say. "I wouldn't want to mess this up."

"No problem!" Pop says enthusiastically. "Blowing bubbles is what I do best."

She whips out a bubble wand and begins to slowly blow a huge bubble.

"I'll make a bubble around me and float out to the crate," she says. The bubble forms all around her and she smiles as she bounces around inside.

Pop begins to float away when a strong wind suddenly kicks up and carries her into the ocean. Her bubble pops, and she splashes into the water. The choppy waves thrash her around.

"Help!" she yells.

"I'll get her!" Loop cries. She twirls her rope in a circle and then throws it out to Pop. But the strong wind whips the rope out of reach.

Something comes over you. You're not scared anymore. You have to save Pop. You put on your propeller cap and fly into the wind.

"Hang on! I'm coming!" you shout.

Your green puffle instincts kick in, and you

steer into the wind. You see Loop's rope bobbing in the water and yell for Pop to grab it.

Pop grabs onto one end, and you dive down and grab the other end. Then you fly back to shore, pulling Pop behind you.

"You saved me!" Pop cries, thankfully.

Bouncer nods out to sea. "The penguin! She's fallen off the crate!"

You follow her gaze and see the penguin flailing to stay afloat. This doesn't look good.

"We need a new plan," Bouncer says.

"PJ, can you use the Aqua Grabber?" you ask referring to the submarine-like device that resides at the Iceberg.

"I think so," PJ says. He waddles over to it and tries the door. "It's stuck!"

"I'll check it out," Flare says. "Locking mechanism's bent. No prob."

Flare whips out his welding torch and has the door to the Aqua Grabber open in seconds. PJ jumps inside and the mini-submarine sinks beneath the waves.

You all watch breathlessly from shore as the green penguin sinks beneath the churning waves. Can PJ save her?

Then the clear dome of the Aqua Grabber pops up, bobbing on top of the choppy waves. The machine's metal claw safely pulls the green penguin out of the water.

PJ steers to shore and drops the penguin onto the Iceberg. She's stunned, but okay.

"I don't know who you all are, but I can't thank you enough," she says. "I fell asleep on the Beach and got washed away by a big wave. If you guys hadn't saved me, I'd probably be floating away to some distant island."

The green penguin leaves the Iceberg. Bouncer hops toward you.

"Thanks for your help," he says. "We couldn't have completed this without you."

"I'm glad to help," you say. "It's good to know you guys are here on Club Penguin, keeping things safe for everyone. But I really should be going now. PJ and I need to find a way to switch back into our bodies."

"I hope it works out," Bouncer says. "If anyone can fix your problem, Gary's the one."

Go to page 21.

CONTINUED FROM PAGE 36.

"Flare!" Blast cries out.

The wind has picked up debris from the beach. A rope has caught the top of the Beacon. It's tangled around Flare, and he's trapped.

You don't think twice. You quickly don your propeller hat and fly against the wind to Flare. When you reach the top of the Beacon, you pull on the rope, setting Flare free.

"Dude, that was gnarly," he says. "I gotta give you mad props for that."

"You'd make a great puffle," says Blast.

Blast's compliment makes you feel really proud. You, Blast, and PJ make a wall around Flare while he works so the wind won't blow him away again. Soon, Flare hops back.

"Hit the switch," he says.

Blast hops on the switch, and the Beacon shines so brightly, you have to turn away.

Flare hops back on his skateboard. He jumps up onto the railing that leads back into the Lighthouse.

"You dudes are cool," he says. "Later."

Flares skates away, riding the railing down

to the Lighthouse floor. Blast is looking through the telescope again.

"The *Migrator* has landed!" he cries.

You and Blast rush to the bottom of the Lighthouse and head outside. Gary is there, along with Captain Rockhopper and Yarr.

"Blast! It's mighty good to see ye, me hearty!" Rockhopper says.

"Ahoy there, old friend!" Yarr says.

As Blast tells Yarr how you all fixed the Beacon, Gary approaches you and PJ.

"I've been looking for you," he says. "I have bad news. The Monster Maker is malfunctioning. It may take days to fix."

"That's all right," you say. "We can wait."

Rockhopper overhears Gary telling you about your predicament. "I may have a remedy for ye, but I'm not sure if it will work," he says.

If you decide to wait for Gary to fix the Monster Maker, go to page 58.

If you let Rockhopper help, go to page 75.

CONTINUED FROM PAGE 52.

You can't resist the chance to help the Elite Puffles. "What's the mission?" you ask.

"In the last few hours, there have been reports of something mysterious floating in the waters off Club Penguin," Bouncer explains.

Chirp shivers. "Some penguins say it's a terrifying sea monster!"

"We won't know what it is until we investigate," Bouncer says. "We've got to get to a high place and scan the waters."

"We'll get a mighty fine view from the Ski Hill," says Blast, the red puffle.

Loop hops over to you. "I'm glad you can join us. Our friend Flit is on a solo mission. He's a green puffle, too. Flit's flying comes in handy on our missions. Now you can fly for us!"

"Uh, sure," you say nervously. You're not sure if you know how to use PJ's propeller hat. But maybe it'll just come naturally.

"What are we waiting for? Let's go!" Pop cries out. She bounces out of the Forest, and you and the rest of the EPF follow her.

You all hop on the Ski Lift and take it to the

top of the Ski Hill. When you get to the top, the puffles spread out, looking over the edge.

"We need a better view," says Blast.

Loop looks at you. "Can you fly to the top of the signpost? You'll get a great view up there!"

You look up at the tall wood pole with signs on top pointing to the different ski trails. From down here, it looks very high.

"Uh, sure!" you say. You put on PJ's propeller hat, the propeller starts to spin, and your puffle tummy lurches as it lifts you into the air.

"Awesome!" you yell. "I'm flying!"

You're flying—but you have no idea how to control your flight path. You dart around the signpost, but you can't get to the top. Then you slam into a snow bank with a crash. You don't know what you were thinking, trying to help the EPF. You should resume your search for Gary.

If you stick with the EPF, go to page 25.

If you run off, go to page 29.

CONTINUED FROM PAGE 40.

You and Bouncer take the tunnel on the right. It's so dark! You can barely see in front of you as you come to another fork in the path.

"Left or right?" you ask.

"Right again, I guess," Bouncer says.

You turn right and follow the winding path.

"It's like some kind of maze," you remark.

Bouncer agrees. "I think we entered the wrong tunnel in the beginning. We should go back to the cave entrance."

You turn around and head back down the passage, quickly reaching another turn.

"Did we go left or right here?" you ask.

"I don't remember. Let's try one and see."

You make a turn and keep going. It gets you nowhere.

"Oh no!" you cry. "We're lost!"

Bouncer stays cool. "We just have to keep trying. We'll get out eventually."

Bouncer must be right, you think as you follow her. *At least, I hope she is!*

THE END

CONTINUED FROM PAGE 71.

You're curious about what Rockhopper's solution might be.

"Let's give it a try," you say.

Rockhopper takes you aboard his quarters in the *Migrator*. He opens up a treasure chest and takes out a piece of bumpy, purple fruit.

"This grows on the shores of a far-off island," he tells you. "The islanders say it has mysterious powers. Why don't ye and yer penguin here take a bite and see if it switches ye back?"

"Interesting," Gary says. "However, I would recommend testing the chemical properties of the fruit in my lab first."

"I'm not afraid," you say. "After all, what could be weirder than what's already happened?"

PJ takes a bite of the fruit and then gives it to you so you can take a bite. You start to feel tingly all over. It must be working!

That's when you notice—strange bumps are popping up all over your skin. You're turning purple, too! You look at PJ, and see the same thing happening to him.

"Well, sink me!" Rockhopper exclaims. "The two of ye look just like the fruit."

"Fascinating," Gary says. "But not the desired result."

Rockhopper pats you on your bumpy head. "No worries, lads. We can set sail for the island right away. The islanders will know what to do, or me name isn't Rockhopper!"

"Welcome aboard, matey!" Yarr tells you.

You are excited to be traveling aboard the *Migrator* with Captain Rockhopper and Yarr. But you're a little nervous, too. It's kind of fun being a puffle, but being a weird, bumpy puffle is a different story. You just hope Rockhopper can help you set things right!

THE END

CONTINUED FROM PAGE 66.

"Try going from three to four," you say.

Bouncer whips up twelve snowballs and throws them around the circle clockwise.

The crystals in the cave glow brighter. Your body tingles. You're a penguin again!

"It worked!" you shout. "Thanks, Bouncer!"

Bouncer looks at you and smiles. But sadly, you can't understand puffle language anymore.

You realize PJ must be a puffle again. Where is he? Finally, it hits you. "When he switched back, he probably went to the igloo."

"Would you like to visit my igloo and meet PJ?" you ask Bouncer. He nods.

Back at your igloo, you find PJ playing with his puffle furniture. He's happy to see you.

"That was quite an adventure, PJ," you say. "I made a new friend. This is Bouncer."

Bouncer and PJ happily play together. You know that Bouncer can't live with you, but you hope she'll come and visit again!

THE END

CONTINUED FROM PAGE 16.

You don't really like the idea of PJ roaming around Club Penguin in your body. You decide to follow PJ and then go look for Gary.

You and Bouncer hop toward the Ice Rink, right down the path from the Snow Forts. Penguins in red and blue jerseys are playing a game of ice hockey, but you don't see PJ!

As you head down another path, your stomach begins to rumble. You are so hungry! The rumbling is so loud that Bouncer hears it.

"Your penguin forgot to feed you?" she asks.

You nod, feeling a little guilty. *You* are the one who forgot to feed PJ back in your igloo. You vow never to forget to feed your puffle again.

"Don't worry," she says. "There's a big bunch of Puffle-O Berry bushes nearby. Follow me."

Bouncer leads you up a small, snowy hill. You see the bushes on the other side, but no Puffle-O Berries on them. A small group of puffles are gathered by the bushes. They look upset.

"What happened here?" Bouncer asks.

"We don't know," answers a pink puffle. "When we got here, the berries were gone."

"Don't worry," Bouncer tells the wild puffles. "I'll help you figure out what happened."

She sounds confident and determined. As she starts to examine the snow for clues, you get the sense that Bouncer is not an ordinary puffle.

You hop alongside Bouncer, and you notice some strange tracks in the snow. It looks like something big was dragged across the ground.

Bouncer examines them. "Excellent! This is a great clue. We should follow the tracks."

You feel proud that you spotted the tracks. You start to hop along the trail when suddenly, a green puffle whizzes by you. He's wearing a propeller hat just like yours, and he's giggling.

"Heads up!" the green puffle calls out.

"Hmm," Bouncer says. "That's Flit. He loves to play tricks. I wonder if he is behind the missing Puffle-O Berries."

Flit is flying in the opposite direction of the tracks—should you follow the tracks, or follow the mischievous puffle, Flit?

If you follow the tracks, go to page 32.
If you follow Flit, go to page 41.

CONTINUED FROM PAGE 13.

When you get to Gary's workshop, he clips a small black box to the pocket of his lab coat.

"It's a puffle translator," he says, looking at you. "Now I can understand both of you."

"That's great," you say with relief. "What happened is weird. Can you change us back?"

"I think I can," Gary says. "But I have another proposition for you. What you two are experiencing is a rare scientific opportunity. I would love to study you both for awhile before I change you back. Would you be interested?"

You and PJ look at each other.

"Gary is awesome," you say. "It would be cool to help him out."

"Definitely," PJ agrees. "Why not?"

So you and PJ move into Gary's workshop. You're really excited—you're pretty sure no other penguin has done that before! You can't wait to get started with Gary's experiments. Switching bodies with your puffle is the most exciting thing that's ever happened to you!

THE END